every book,
every page,
SOMETHING
happens!

Printed in U.S.A. © 1997 Scholastic Book Fairs, Inc.

A Gift For :
Archbishop Neale School
Given By : The Murphy Family **Scholastic Book Fairs®**

14985 EN
Dog Heaven

Rylant, Cynthia
ATOS BL 3.4
Points: 0.5   LG

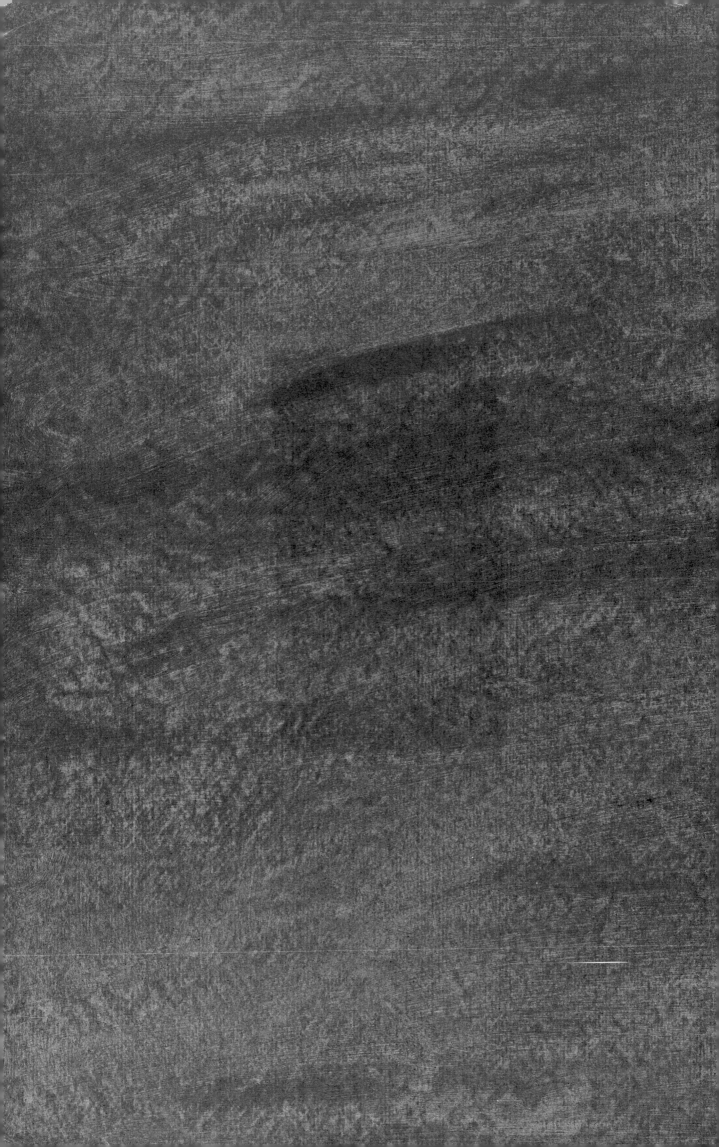

WRITTEN AND ILLUSTRATED BY

Cynthia Rylant

SCHOLASTIC INC.

New York   Toronto   London   Auckland   Sydney

DOG

HEAVEN

This book was originally published in hardcover by the Blue Sky
Press in 1995.

ISBN 0-590-41702-9

12 11 10 9 8 7 6   8 9/9 0 1 2 3/0

Printed in the U.S.A.   08

FOR DIANE

When dogs go to Heaven,
they don't need wings
because God knows that
dogs love running best.

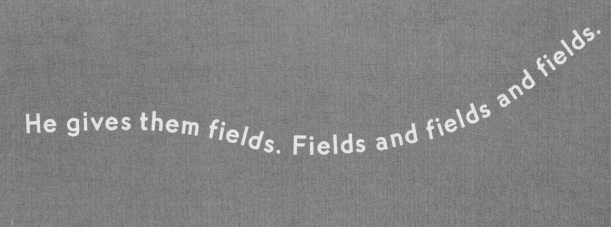

He gives them fields. Fields and fields and fields.

When a dog first arrives in Heaven,

he just runs.

Dog Heaven has clear, wide lakes
filled with geese who honk and flap
and tease. The dogs love this.

They run beside the water and bark
and bark and God watches them
from behind a tree and smiles.

There are children,
of course.
Angel children.

God knows that dogs love children more than anything else in the world, so He fills Dog Heaven with plenty of them. There are children on bikes and children on sleds. There are children throwing red rubber balls and children pulling kites through the clouds. The dogs are there, and the children love them dearly.

And, oh,
the dog biscuits.
Biscuits and biscuits
as far as the eye can see.

God has a sense of humor, so He makes His
biscuits in funny shapes for His dogs. There
are kitty-cat biscuits and squirrel biscuits.
Ice-cream biscuits and ham-sandwich biscuits.

Every angel who passes by
has a biscuit for a dog.

And, of course, all God's dogs
sit when the angels say "sit."

Every dog becomes a good
dog in Dog Heaven.

God turns
clouds inside out to
make fluffy beds for the dogs
in Dog Heaven, and when they
are tired from running and
barking and eating ham-
sandwich biscuits,

the dogs each find a cloud
bed for sleeping.

They turn around and
around in the cloud...

...until it feels just right,
and then they curl up

and they sleep.

God watches over each one of them and there are no bad dreams.

Dogs in Dog Heaven
have almost always
belonged to somebody
on Earth and, of course,
the dogs remember this.
Heaven is full of memories.

So sometimes an angel will walk a dog
back to Earth for a little visit and quietly,
invisibly, the dog will sniff about his old
backyard, will investigate the cat next
door, will follow the child to school, will
sit on the front porch and wait for the mail.

When he is satisfied

that all is well, the dog

will return to Heaven with the angel.

It is where dogs belong,

near God who made them.

The dogs in Dog Heaven who
had no real homes on Earth
are given one in Heaven.

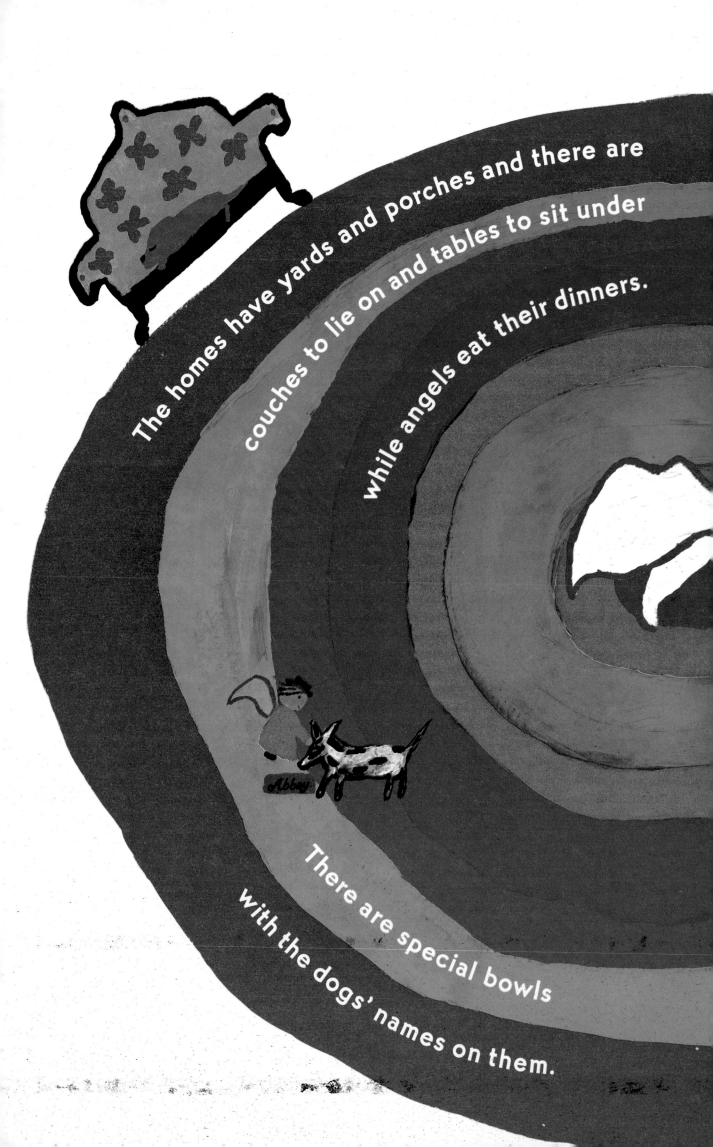

The homes have yards and porches and there are couches to lie on and tables to sit under while angels eat their dinners.

There are special bowls with the dogs' names on them.

And each dog is petted and reminded

how good he is, all day long.

Dogs in Dog Heaven may stay as long as
they like and this can mean forever.

They will be there when old friends show up. They will be there at the door.

Angel dogs.

The paintings in this book

were done with acrylics.

The text type was set in Martin Gothic Bold

and the display type in LoType Medium

by WLCR New York, Inc.

Color separations were made by

Bright Arts, Ltd., Singapore.

Original Blue Sky Press edition

designed by Kathleen Westray

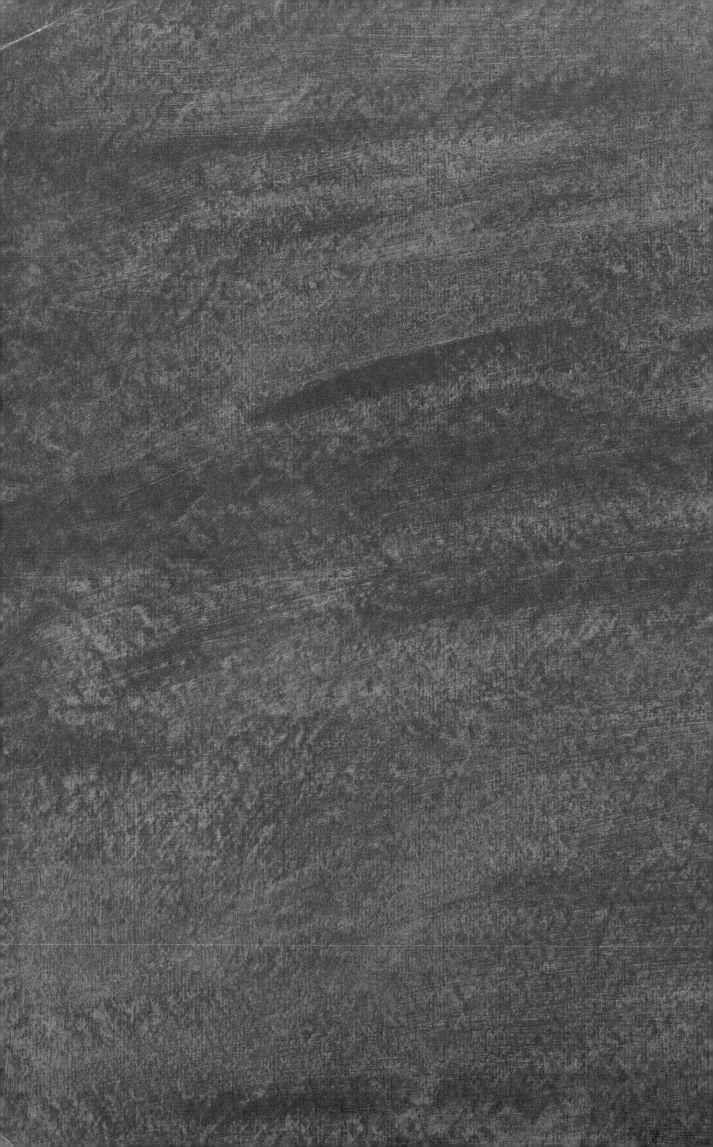